3 0132 02368805 9

D0717499

NORTHUMBERLAND COUNTY LIBRARY

You should return this book on or before the last date sta
below unless an extension of the loan period is granted.

Application for renewal may be made by letter or telephone

Lilli~Pilli's Sister

Anna Branford

≈ *Illustrated by* ≈
LINDA CATCHLOVE

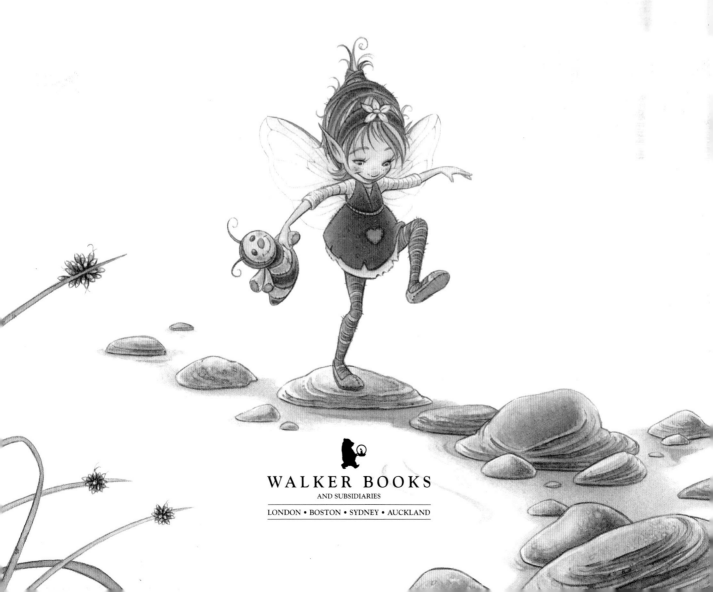

WALKER BOOKS
AND SUBSIDIARIES

LONDON • BOSTON • SYDNEY • AUCKLAND

Beside a stream that swoops and pours in the rainy season, and slows to a muddy trickle in the dry season, a small fairy called Lilli-Pilli is helping her dad to make a cradle for a new baby fairy.

They are sanding a curl of
tree bark to make the edges
smooth and safe.

"Will it be the right size for my
sister to sleep in when she's born?"
asks Lilli-Pilli.

"It might be a bit wide, but it
will have to do," sighs Dad. "And
remember, we don't know if it's a
sister or a brother just yet."

"It's a sister," says Lilli-Pilli.

Lilli-Pilli goes inside to tell Mum about the bark-curl cradle being a bit wide, but Mum only opens one eye very slightly. These days her tummy is so huge and round that when she tries to fly, her feet hardly leave the ground.

"I hope my sister is born soon," says Lilli-Pilli. "I need someone to play with."

"What if the baby is a boy?" asks Mum, sleepily. "You'll still play with the baby if it's a brother, won't you?"

"I'll still play with the baby if it's a mosquito," says Lilli-Pilli. "But I'm definitely going to have a sister. I can feel it in my wings."

"Either way," yawns Mum, "we'll need something soft to put inside the cradle, especially if it's a bit wide. Why don't you see what you can find?"

Lilli-Pilli flies all the way to the top
of the great gnarled tree to ask the
kingfisher for a feather.

"I need something soft to go inside
my sister's cradle," she explains.

"Of course. I'll give you a feather," chuckles the kingfisher. "But are you sure it's a sister? I think I feel a brother in my wings."

"I'm *pretty* sure," says Lilli-Pilli. But actually she feels a little less sure. The kingfisher's wings are not often wrong.

With the feather tucked under her
arm, Lilli-Pilli flies over to the grasses
to ask the patterned yellow moth for
one of her empty cocoons.

"I need something soft to go
inside my sister's cradle," she explains.

"Of course. I'll give you a cocoon," whispers the moth. "But are you certain it's a sister? I think I feel a brother in my wings."

"I'm *fairly* certain," says Lilli-Pilli. But she feels even less certain. The patterned yellow moth's wings are almost always right.

With the feather and the soft cocoon tucked under her arm, Lilli-Pilli flies up into the low branches of the river tree to ask the white-winged flycatcher for a small nest.

"I need something soft to go inside my sister's cradle," she explains.

"Of course. You can have a nest," chirrups the white-winged flycatcher.

"But are you positive it's a sister?
I think I feel a brother in my wings."

The white-winged flycatcher's wings have
never made a mistake before.

Lilli-Pilli sighs. "I *thought* I was positive.
But maybe I was wrong."

A feather, a cocoon and a nest is rather a lot for a small fairy to fly home with.

Lilli-Pilli flies slowly. She had been looking forward to having a sister.

As she gets closer, she hears some strange squeaking, squawking noises coming from home, like small magpies calling for their parents.

When she flies through the front door, Mum is holding a squeaking bundle. Lilli-Pilli gives her the soft cocoon and Mum tucks a tiny baby fairy snugly inside.

"Is it a brother or a sister?" whispers Lilli-Pilli.

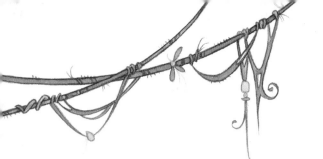

"It's a brother," says Mum.

"He's beautiful," says Lilli-Pilli, softly.

But there is squawking coming from another little bundle that Dad is holding. Lilli-Pilli gives Dad the small nest and *he* tucks another tiny baby fairy snugly inside.

"Two babies!" squeaks Lilli-Pilli, so surprised that she forgets to whisper.

Mum puts the twins in the cradle (which is just the right size for two) and Dad digs the spike of the kingfisher's feather into the ground so that it curves over the cradle like a shade.

Lilli-Pilli rocks the bark-curl very gently and the babies stop squeaking and squawking.

"Are they both brothers?" asks
Lilli-Pilli.

"A brother and a sister,"
whispers Dad.

"They're *perfect*," says Lilli-Pilli.
"All our wings were right."

For my brilliant godson, Louis. Love Anna x AB
For my gorgeous girl, Lily. Love Mum x LC

First published 2014 by Walker Books Ltd
87 Vauxhall Walk, London SE11 5HJ

10 9 8 7 6 5 4 3 2 1

Text © 2014 Anna Branford
Illustrations © 2014 Linda Catchlove

The right of Anna Branford and Linda Catchlove to be identified as
author and illustrator respectively of this work has been asserted by
them in accordance with the Copyright, Designs and Patents Act 1988

This book has been typeset in Goudy Oldstyle

Printed in China

All rights reserved. No part of this book may be reproduced, transmitted or
stored in an information retrieval system in any form or by any means,
graphic, electronic or mechanical, including photocopying, taping
and recording, without prior written permission from the publisher.

British Library Cataloguing in Publication Data:
a catalogue record for this book is available from the British Library

ISBN 978-1-4063-5354-9

www.walker.co.uk